Claire Streaks

Through the Autumn of Her Life

Claire Streaks Through the Autumn of Her Life

by Rose Baldwin

SENESCERE

Rancho Mirage, California

Parts of this book have been published before. A version of *The Guy From San Bernardino* appeared in the anthology *San Bernardino, Singing* edited by Nikia Chaney. *Resistance Failed* appeared in *Straitjackets Magazine.* Several poems and stories appeared in *Cholla Needles* and/or have been read at the open mics they sponsor.

Published in 2021
Printed in the United States of America

ISBN 978-0-9981390-3-6
SENESCERE. Rancho Mirage, California

*This book would not exist
without the encouragement,
advice and help from everyone at
Cholla Needles Arts and
Literary Library.
Thank you.*

CONTENTS

Introduction..7

Claire Learns to be Old 11

Resistance Failed..17

Claire Makes New Friends 18

Life 31

Claire Remembers..32

The Guy From San Bernardino 41

Bill's Story 44

Piper's Poem...57

Carl's Story 59

An Old Man's Poem 67

Claire and the Mementos..............................69

Mementos...80

Stories of Wonder and Magic.......................81

Sunrise..91

Claire Attends an Open Mic.........................92

Open Mic..97

Phyllis's Story 99

INTRODUCTION

Though it's only been a few years since she moved from Wisconsin to Palm Springs, Claire Wilson considers herself a Californian. But when she calls a light evening meal supper, other Californians say she talks like a Midwesterner. She wonders how they can call popcorn, and three vodkas, dinner.

The praise Claire received for her chapbook *The Claire Stories* motivated her to write more stories and poems about herself and the people around her. She wrote:

> I sit down and write a poem
> when lonely mad or sad
> for in the quiet of that work
> my scarred heart can laugh

Her dog-owning neighbor, who rarely picked up her pup's waste, was critical of her poems saying they were dumb and silly, of no significance or value. To test their worth, Claire wrote this poem just for that neighbor:

When my neighbor's poodle
on my lawn did sh*t
I wrote a little verse
instead of throw a fit

The small poem fit nicely into a corner of her HOA's newsletter. Everyone in the community read it and recognized just who it was about. Her neighbor never spoke to her again, and her dog never used Claire's lawn again, either. That was enough for Claire.

Feeling invincible, Claire wrote this poem about another neighbor:

When I crossed the street too slow
and that driver yelled a zinger
all that I did think about
was words that rhyme with finger

When that poem was published in the HOA's newsletter, again, everyone in the community recognized who it was about. Though the embarrassment wasn't enough to stop his cursing, or his reckless driving, he was known forever after as Finger.

Everyone was happy when he moved to an assisted living facility. A woman from Chicago bought his condo—she took it "as is" and got a real bargain.

Claire Learns to be Old

It took many lessons for Claire to accept her own aging and eventually learn how to be old. To be fair, it isn't as easy as most people think.

Her first notable lesson came when she was thirty-five or six. At the hardware store, a cute clerk started flirting. She thought he was younger than her, but not **so** young, and anyway, he started it and then went on and on teasing her about her do-it-yourself project. Finally, she suggested that if he so doubted her skills, he should come to her house and help with the work. That's when he struck.

"It's amazing," he said. "You remind me so much of my mother."

It felt like a gut punch and her face showed it.

"No, no, no, no, no," he said. "My mother is real young. She was only fifteen when I was born. And she's pretty; really, really pretty." As if anything he could say would restore that playful mood.

Over time there were other incidents. Young women said things, harmless things, really, such as: "I used to have one of those when they were in style, I loved it," not knowing they were referring to her most recent purchase which Claire considered quite stylish; or, worse, "gosh, I bet you were pretty, when you were young;" or, her least favorite, "I hope I look like you, when I'm old." Claire knew they likely intended to flatter, but the comments made her aware that her notion of herself probably wasn't accurate. Sometimes she could almost laugh about it but more often the comments stung.

Then came the birthday when even she was shocked to realize how old she'd gotten—it seemed impossible. Later that same week her new doctor, (a woman young enough to be her granddaughter), confirms it by giving her advice on how to maintain "vitality and health," a phrase that in her mind was only used with old people—exercise, the doctor said, is important.

At the gym Claire squarely confronts limitations that have come on so gradually, she'd been unaware of them. While young women managed to maintain taut muscles by jumping on an elliptical machine for a few minutes, doing a few crunches and a couple squats, she worked out diligently with little visible result.

The weightlifters were nice to her. A couple of them commented on her persistence, without mentioning the five-pound weights she used or her need to hold on to something for balance. One older fella even suggested Claire join he and his girlfriend for a three-way. Though she did not pursue the opportunity, she was grateful for the offer—it had been a long time since she'd received such a proposition.

To be honest, Claire enjoyed the man's easy banter and flirtatiousness. The attention and the fact that she could walk up and down stairs without getting winded or feeling as if she was going to fall kept her going to the gym. That she was able to open jars unaided, while many of her friends needed gadgets to assist them, was a bonus.

It was at the end of a writing workshop that she accepted that she was old. Claire knew she was being patronized when at her wrap-up meeting the teacher called her work "sweet." The poem she'd written for the workshop was about a long-suffering, woman who stabbed her husband...twenty-seven times...while he slept—hardly a sweet topic, even if the poem did rhyme. As the conversation finished, the teacher added insult to injury by professing her admiration for Claire's "spunkiness" and pronouncing Claire her "adopted mother."

Yes, that was the day Claire accepted that people saw her as old. For, though she wanted to say, "If you were my daughter, I'd tell you to lose some weight and get a decent bra," she didn't. A calm knowing settled over her and she was silent. She felt her mouth curl into a new sort of smile. Even without a mirror she knew she was wearing a look she'd seen many times on others and interpreted as a sweet, old-lady look. At last she understood it isn't sweet at all, but, is, instead, about knowing that time has a way of settling scores. Yes, Claire knew, that teacher would get hers', as we all do, one way or the other.

After that, Claire felt ready to go to the senior center where she hoped she might find others who knew that too.

Resistance Failed

I've become my mother
I see it in the mirror
I've got her jowls and waddle
her belly and her rear

I do the things she did
and even use her words
my hopes my dreams my fears
are very much like hers

Though we rarely did agree
and barely liked each other
resistance failed us both, and
I've become my mother

Claire Makes New Friends

Before visiting the senior center, Claire had steeled herself for the possibility that it would be full of old people, doddering and dottie, but that is not the case. Yes, there are some with canes or walkers, a few have their feet shoved into big boots to protect fragile or healing bones, but, for the most part the people look like her—some even look younger than her.

There is a large cluster of people dressed in athletic gear, standing near the entrance, and looking ready to hike or bike, to play tennis or golf. They don't seem to mix, even within their group. Claire sees no one wearing cross-trainers talking to someone wearing hiking boots, or anyone in a tennis outfit talking to someone in a golf shirt, let alone one of the athletic people talking with a walker-using person. Many of the sports people look at Claire (as she is looking at them) and then quickly away. She figures they have (correctly) identified her as not one of their ilk.

Apart from the athletes there is an assortment of less easily pigeonholed folks. The women are as different from each other as can be, ranging from large-robust and pink-faced to tiny and grey. Their clothes range from subtle-stylish to flashy. Regardless of their style, most are dressed comfortably.

The men are less varied, most wear khaki pants and a shirt with a button down collar. Many have rounded bellies some of which hang over belt buckles. Liver spots are prominent on the men's faces and hands. Claire guesses make-up and minor cosmetic surgery is the reason the women display fewer of these marks.

Claire joins a group touring the facility. In addition to the greeting hall, administrative offices and library, there is a lunch room setup with metal stackable chairs around round folding tables, and three classrooms, all similarly furnished. In the first classroom the chairs form a circle, yoga mats and foam exercise aids are stacked along the wall along with long folding tables; in another the chairs are behind long rectangular folding tables lined up so the occupants all faced front; and, in a third larger room, that has a sign on the door indicating it is called the lecture hall, the chairs are arranged in rows facing a podium, both round and rectangular folded tables lean against the wall. Claire notes the rooms are separated by sliding panels that allow them to be combined, but the wear pattern in the carpet suggests that is rarely done.

A schedule showing the classes and activities that are offered is taped to the door of each room. As the tour ends Claire ducks into a memoir writing class, that is just starting. She immediately likes the teacher and thinks the stories people tell will inspire her. She decides she will join the class for future meetings.

As she is preparing to leave, two women introduce themselves. Ronnie is a widow with a grown daughter and, though, she had spent all of her life until three years ago in Hollywood (her husband had worked in the movie industry, though never on camera), has such a sweetness and simple comeliness about her that she might have posed for a picture of a Swiss milk maid.

The second woman, Stanley, has lived in several different cities in the U. S. and a couple other countries; admits to being thrice married and divorced. She dresses in men's clothes, wears her grey-hair short (and mostly uncombed), has weathered skin and a gravelly voice that suggest mischief and at least a couple decades of heavy smoking.

The three talk easily and there is general sense of delight when the pair confirms that Claire lives in same senior's community as them. She agrees to meet them later that afternoon and walk to a local bar/restaurant for the happy hour special.

They are among the bar's earliest arrivals, only having been preceded by a couple day drinkers. The women settle around a table close enough to the bar, and the television mounted behind it, that they can hear the early edition of the news. They learn there's been a fire, an auto accident, and a Dalmatian, named Spots, owned by a man who suffers from dementia, is missing—all residents are asked to be on the lookout for the dog.

Three sips into their first glass of wine, Claire turns toward Stanley, "So, how did you get your name?"

"It's a simple story," Stanley says. "I have two older sisters. When I was born, my parents were told I would be their last child. My father had wanted a son but had to settle for a girl named after him. He was thrilled when I turned out to be a tomboy. He'd been athletic and my interest in sports gave him someone to teach what he knew."

She changes the subject by asking both of her tablemates, "So, what story do you want to tell?" referring to the assignment given in the memoir writing class. "Or do you need to think about it?"

"I knew someone would ask that," Ronnie says. "And no I do not need to think about it."

She takes a deep breath. "Lately I've wondered what my life would have been if I hadn't gotten pregnant. Don't get me wrong, I've had a good life. I love my daughter and I loved my husband. We were good together. But we got married because I was pregnant. We both attended the local state college so our parents, his and mine, were available to help us. They were great. They chipped in so we had a place to live and took turns babysitting. I wonder—that's all."

"Did you consider other options?" Claire says.

"Abortion? Oh, no! I already thought that God was punishing me and that I de-served to have my dreams clipped—that seems so outdated now. I hadn't even tried to get birth control pills when we started having sex, because I thought only a bad girl would use them. I was afraid my mother would find out."

"The things we do to please our mothers…," Stanley says.

Ronnie cuts her off. "Before I knew I was pregnant, I'd gotten a scholarship to go to Barnard and my husband was going to go to Berkley. Both he and I accepted the change in our lives. But just before she died, my mother told me she always wondered why I didn't terminate the pregnancy, and said that she would have. And, since then, I sometimes wonder, what if…?"

"Wow, that's huge!" Claire says.

"Really?" Ronnie says. "You probably wonder sometimes if you should have had children."

"No. I don't. That was one of my best

decisions. The most nagging regret I have is a tiny and mischievous thing."

"Tell us," Stanley says.

Claire smiles and nods. "When I was a young girl I dated an actor," she says. "To earn money he emceed strip shows that were put on between the movies at this seedy theater. One day two of the dancers were late for the show. The third, pointed out that I would fit into either of the absent dancer's costumes and that they were in the dressing room. Since the show could be put on with two girls, my willingness to dance would have solved the problem. She assured me that it wasn't hard and since I'd seen the show many times that I could fake it. I said no. Eventually the girls showed up. I knew when they walked in that I'd made a mistake though I didn't realize I'd still regret it as an old woman—I would love to know what it's like to walk out on a stage, undress, and hear people cheer."

"Why didn't you do it?" Ronnie says.

"You wouldn't guess it to look at me now, but, as a young woman, I was thin and flat chested. I was afraid someone would laugh at me."

"Claire! That's a terrible, sad story! I'm sure you were beautiful," Stanley says. "But, you know, I have a regret that's a lot like that."

"Let's hear it," Claire says.

"One day I was on this stretch of beach north of Santa Barbara with a man I almost married, gosh, I wonder what ever happened to him," Stanley says. "Anyway, we could see a long way in both directions and knew we were the only people on the beach. I wanted to skinny dip, so we did. It was divine. I loved the feel of the cold water on me and the way it flowed over my body. Then, we lay naked on the beach and I felt the sun all over me. I remember it as if it was yesterday. That fella, jeesh, I can't even remember what he looked like, anyway, he was on the blanket next to me and he rolled onto his side and kissed me. I'm certain he wanted to have sex. I stopped him."

"Why?" Claire asked.

"I don't even know. It just seemed wrong. I guess I was afraid of being caught. I never had another chance to have sex on a beach and I think of what I missed every time I see a picture of one. It makes me wonder what other harmless opportunities I turned down for no good reason."

The bartender brought them a second drink and each of them lifted their glass and took a sip. Ronnie noticed that they were drinking in sync.

"We're sort of the happy hour drill team," she says indicating with a hand gesture what she was referring to. They laugh and take another sip in unison, and then another and they laugh again.

"So, are those the stories you'll write up for the class?" Ronnie says.

Claire shrugs.

"No," Stanley says. "You know that skinny woman, with the red hair, is likely to tell everyone they can still do anything they want, that, "age is only a number." It's what she always says—even when the notion is preposterous. Can you imagine me splayed on a beach at this age?"

"Or me taking my clothes off on stage?!" Claire says.

"God knows what she'd do with an admission like mine," Ronnie says.

They each have a prime rib slider and a small salad, and finish about the time the bar starts to get busy. They walk the short distance home, in the last of the twilight, keeping an eye out for the missing dog, but they don't see him.

"Wouldn't it be something if that poor man with dementia lost his dog long ago and just now thought to look for him?" Claire says.

Life

It's all about the people
you meet out on the street
some are mean and cranky
others are real sweet

but each one has a story
their personal tale to tell
about the mountains that they climbed
or the heights from which they fell

the story comes in chapters
about choices that were made
characters who came and went
and those who came and stayed

Claire Remembers

After her happy-hour supper and the conversation with Ronnie and Stanley about the past, Claire's mind is full of memories. She thinks about her aunt Maddie who everyone in the family said, with sadness, that she was like. While they lamented that Claire was tall, and bookish, she was delighted to be like Maddie who had a job and boyfriends, drove a sports car and traveled. Maddie had even gone to Europe—a barely imaginable adventure to the young Claire.

Maddie told her that being different was all right. At the same time, she warned Claire that being herself might not be easy and, lest Claire think she could pretend ordinariness, Maddie told her being different, with all its challenges, would be easier, for her, than trying to fit in. Later, when Claire wasn't invited to any of the high school dances, her mother tried to comfort her by saying lots of girls don't go to them. But Maddie told her flat out that it might be hard for her to find a husband because she was smart, independent, and funny; that only very special men enjoyed those qualities in a woman. She told Claire to plan a life for herself, if someone came along who she wanted to share it with, all the better, but she'd be wise to plan on living alone. Maddie assured her that lovers were fairly easy to find and, though it wasn't real love, it could seem like it for a while. She said it could be fun, as long as Claire didn't get her hopes up.

She remembered Maddie's delight when, Claire, already in her forties, and home for her mother's birthday, met sweet-sweet Walt—a large awkward man a few years younger than her who ran his family's farm. She'd known of him when they were children. He told her he'd had a crush on her then but that their four year age difference had been an insurmountable obstacle for him.

He invited her to attend an event with him. She'd accepted, suggesting it would be easier if they met at his house. When she arrived no one answered the door. It being a pleasant afternoon, she sat on the porch and watched the cows graze in the field across the road. Shortly, she heard the sound of running feet on gravel and a man's anguished cries, "Damn, damn, damn." She turned and saw him hurrying toward her. He wore rubber boots and overalls with a plaid flannel shirt.

"Claire, I'm so, so, sorry," he said. "I got distracted. They're hatching—the chicks, wanna see?" She did. So he led her to one of the smaller outbuildings and the two of them watched chicks peck their way out of their shells.

"There are only a few eggs left to hatch, do you mind if we wait for them?" he said. She did not. She watched as this hulk of a man gently took each newly hatched chick to a fenced circle with heat lamps over it and was astonished that they walked immediately and then ate as soon as they found the food.

After all the eggs had hatched he said, "Have you ever seen cows milked?" She had not. He showed her the milking salon, where two men worked. He let her taste milk drawn that morning and chilled. "Oh, my god," she'd exclaimed when it coated her mouth.

"Yeah, we think of the whole milk in the store as low fat," he'd said.

He showed her a huge building with bins of cotton seed and enormous pieces of farm equipment. He took her to a barn and showed her cows that would be shown at the next county fair.

Instead of the barbecue they'd planned to attend, they warmed a frozen pizza and took it, and a six pack of beer, to the building with the new chicks. Walt set up two chaise lounges and they ate and watched the hatchlings. He told her about chickens and the county fair; she fell asleep listening, and slept through to morning. Waking she found she was covered with a homemade afghan that smelled of lilacs. Walt stood over her holding a large mug of coffee—he'd already been awake for hours and performed the morning milking. Then, in the conversation that would change her life, she told him things there had never been anyone to talk to about, and he didn't laugh or think them odd at all.

She stayed for a week then went back to her home in Los Angeles to consider the offer he'd made to her. She decided to wrap up her affairs and move back to the small town where she'd grown up. When she returned she found he'd rearranged his house to accommodate her—and the changes were exactly what she would have asked for. It was as if he was her other half.

Their relationship was companionable. Even in the beginning they would stop in the middle of having sex because one or the other of them would think of something they wanted to tell the other. After the conversation they would resume, often allowing the need to talk interrupt them again and again. He treated her like a queen and she fell totally in love. They married nine months later.

To the city person she had once been her new life would have seemed small and boring, but in it Claire found contentment. During the years that followed, she helped her mother deal with her father's sickening and to move to an apartment after his death. The two weren't close but Claire knew her help was appreciated. When the time came, she buried her mother next to her father.

Throughout all, her aunt Maddie remained Claire's rock, but with age she became forgetful and disoriented. Finally it was Claire's turn to be in charge. She found a safe place for her aunt to live. It was torture for her to watch Maddie's decline. During her aunt's lucid moments she made it clear that she too knew what was happening to her and was anguished over not being able to stop it.

Walt's sudden and untimely death left her very much at loose ends. Like many family farms, the one she'd lived on for over twenty years, was bequeathed to Walt's male relatives. No one pressured her to leave the house, but it was obviously inconvenient for the nephew who took over the operation to drive in every day. Claire was dismayed that the boy lacked her husband's aesthetic, he was all business and wanted to get rid of the chickens and the flower beds that Walt had loved so much. The boy talked about increasing profitability and started using hormones on the cows—something Walt had vehemently opposed.

By the time Maddie died, Claire was eager to leave. So, she, an aging somewhat odd woman—again alone in the world, went back to California—a place where many people are somewhat odd, and alone.

Talking with Ronnie and Stanley had made her think about all these things. Lately she'd noticed that the smell and feel of the dry California air reminded her of things from before Walt—her old California life, and things that had seemed perfect to someone who hadn't yet known better.

The Guy From San Bernardino

It was many years ago
that I felt so in love
but he's the man who on this day
I am thinking of

I remember how he smelled
and his spasms when he came
but you know for the life of me
I can't think of his name

I remember he was funny
and laughed at my jokes too
smart and sweet he liked to talk
and spin a tale or two

He turned a lot of heads
with his hair so thick and wavy
even though all that is clear,
his name? well, that escapes me

We ate at the Castaways
and danced at the D I
by day we hiked on mountains
at night we searched the sky

How did I let him get away?
that beautiful heart throb
I'd look for him on Google
if. . .wait, was his name Bob?

I thought we'd love forever
and share happiness galore
with slights and hurts we grew apart
until we spoke no more

At the end I felt carved out
my heart wounded and lame
even now I wonder
when I think of what's-his-name

The Castaways is a restaurant and the DI is a popular dance
hall. Both are located in San Bernardino, CA

Bill's Story

At the next memoir writing class, Claire and her friends realize that they needn't have worried about what story they would tell. By the time they arrive more people have signed up to read than can be accommodated in the next three classes. Claire and her friends will remain spectators for a while.

Bill Johnson is first on the list. He tells how while he was packing to move into a seniors' apartment building, he found a story he'd written long ago. It had won first place in a contest run by the government agency where he'd worked; been published in the agency newsletter; posted in the lunchroom; even given to new employees.

He says he was proud of it then and, Claire thinks, since he brought it to read here, (and handed out copies of that original—courier font and all), he still is.

Why I Became a Social Worker
by Bill Johnson

Eddie Smith was an old man nobody liked who lived in a single-wide mobile home a couple streets over from the one I grew up in. When I was in high school, Eddie had a stroke and Social Services arranged for me to sit with him while his wife, Dorothy, went shopping and had her hair done.

The first time I went to see Eddie, I spotted Dorothy standing on her front step from about a half block away. By the time I got to the edge of their lot she'd walked to her car and was backing out of the driveway. She rolled down the window and yelled, "Door's open. There's pop in the fridge," before driving away. After that she just waved. I guess she figured I already knew the drill.

Their place looked about the same as all the others in the community. It had brown shag carpet, dark paneling on the walls and a low ceiling covered in acoustic tile. It smelled stale. Eddie sat curled over onto himself on a sofa with a maroon plaid design just visible around the edges of the old sheet that covered it. "Come in. Come in. And close that door before I get a draft and get sick," he said.

Eddie's stroke had left his right side weak and unpredictable but had not affected his ability to speak. Each time I saw him he began talking as soon as I was in the door and only stopped when he heard Dorothy return.

He talked about FDR and what a good president he'd been leading the country out of the Great Depression and through the Second World War, in which he, Eddie, had served in the Navy. He talked about Frank Sinatra and Benny Goodman and Gene Krupa and Billy Holiday and how they made the best music. He talked about Sandy Koufax and Babe Ruth. He talked about Ovaltine and Horlicks malt tablets in a bottle.

One day he started talking about a dog. "The people who lived next door to my mother-in-law had a Shelty," he said, "full bred, papers and everything, but they didn't take care of her.

"I was sitting on the stoop of my mother-in-law's house and saw the kids chasing that dog around the yard. The mother of the family comes out'a the house and loads the kids into the car and leaves—just like that. She don't tie the dog up or put her in the house or even put water out. Nothin'.

"So the dog sees me sittin' there and comes over and puts her head in my lap. Her fur is matted; she needs a bath. I scratch her ears and under her chin. I give her some water. She loves the attention. You should'a seed the sad look in that dog's eyes. It was like she knew she deserved better but somehow she was where she was.

"So, I'm scratching her back and realize she's pregnant. Jesus H. Christ, I think, she just finished a litter and she has another one on the way. It made me mad. Here they have this really nice dog and no one even thinks to keep her in and breed her proper. They just let her run and the mutts crawl all over her. It's a damned shame when people have nice things and don't take care a them. If that dog had'a been a person no one would blame her for running away. What did they think, the dog would take care of herself?"

Eddie was more riled up than usual so I figured the story was important to him. I didn't understand why. Dorothy came home and he stopped talking and I let it go thinking he could explain it to me another time.

It was only a week or so after that that Eddie had another stroke and died. His wake was held at one of the local funeral homes. There were more people there than I'd expected, all standing around the room in little groups talking and laughing—I think they came for a free meal. I was surprised to see my father sitting with his friends near the door and asked him why he'd come.

"I knew that man a long time," he said. "I sorta' dated one'a his daughters."

As far as I knew then, Eddie had two daughters. They were both divorced, shared a house, and worked at the Walmart. They had a bunch of kids. It seemed funny to think about my father chasing either of them. It made me wonder if they might have been pretty, once.

I walked up to the coffin. Eddie looked small and silly with rouge on his cheeks. Then I went over to

Dorothy and the girls and told them how sorry I was for their loss and then back to my father.

"Which one did you date?" I asked.

"Not one of them," he said. "I dated the one that moved to Memphis. She's s'posed to come."

I knew the minute she got there. The room became quiet and everyone turned to look at her. She resembled her sisters except that she was curved where they were square and solid where they were bulbous. She was dressed in black while Dorothy and the girls were not. She moved smoothly into the room, looked briefly around, then walked to the coffin. As she passed I saw my father's friends poke each other in the ribs and smile.

She knelt in front of the coffin talking quietly to her father's remains, and the men began to move toward her. Finishing, she stood and turned.

"Hello," one of the men said to her.

She nodded but kept walking.

Another man moved into her path. "Remember me?" he said.

She stopped. "This is my father's funeral."

Everyone in the room watched. I heard a woman say, "Her and her wild ways—comin' here."

Then the minister walked in and there was a flurry of activity. The men moved closer to Eddie's daughter. She turned and I saw a terrible scared look in her eyes that seemed to be just like the one Eddie'd described seeing in that dog's eyes and I knew why that story was important. I also realized I could make it a little better. I stepped between my father and his friends and

Eddie Smith's daughter and said, "I was a friend of your father's." Then I put out my arm, like a guy might do in a movie. "May I walk with you?"

She accepted my arm and we took seats behind her mother and sisters, and their children. The minister gave the standard "I don't know this guy but he's dead and someone has to say something" speech. I felt like I should be paying attention but instead I snuck looks at her and around the room. As far as I could tell, she was the only person who cried.

After the eulogy, she turned to me and said, "Are you the boy who sat with my father?"

I nodded.

"You're very nice," she said. "I'm glad my father had a friend like you at the end of his life."

Then she gave me the softest of all possible kisses on my cheek. I felt my face redden. My heart raced. By the time I was able to look up, she was gone. She didn't go to the dinner. I saw a car with Tennessee license plates in her mother's driveway that evening but it was gone in the morning.

It was that story Eddie told me and the look in his daughter's eyes before, and after, I offered her my arm at his funeral that changed my view of life. Because of them, I understood, that no one should have to stand up to the world alone and even a small act of kindness could change everything for the better. That's why I became a Social Worker—to be there for people when they don't have anyone else to protect them.

# # #

Finished, Bill takes a deep breath and smiles. He says that by the time he'd retired, there were no more writing contests and this story, he knows, would surely not have won if there had been one—in his agency, fiscal concerns had become more highly regarded than compassionate ones.

He says he likes being reminded about Eddie Smith, and his daughter; and what a sweet and hopeful young man he had been. Bill tells everyone that he put the story in the expandable file with his important papers, his will and financial information because he wants this story to be how he is remembered.

Claire watches a group of women surround Bill Johnson, showering him with praise. She turns and sees Ronnie is wiping tears off her cheeks. "That is such a sweet story," she says. "What a nice man."

Stanley chuckles. "If that man handles this right, that he'll never have to cook for himself again."

Piper's Poem

One year ago today
my dear mother died
I feel her inspiration
like she's still at my side

She gave me my values and
I thank my mom for that
without her constant harping
I might have gotten fat

She taught me status counts
to get all that I can
that is how I happened
to marry a rich man

I share her zest for life
and her love of gin
tennis in the morning
club lunch with a grin

I thank my mom for saying
what a let-down children are
so I didn't ruin my figure
look good in my sports-car

The one complaint I have
she took so long to go
bills for care had mounted
leaving little to bestow

But I forgive her disregard
the battle fought and lost
I know she wanted to live on
but think about the cost

Carl's Story

Carl isn't Claire's cup of tea and she guesses he feels the same about her—they generally give each other wide berth. He prefers the small girlish women, the ones who cast coy looks at every man and squirm and giggle whenever they're spoken to.

In spite of her distain for the man, Claire gives him credit. On the day he's scheduled to read he manages to bring enough copies of his story for everyone. After handing them out, he stands confidently in front of the group, makes no introduction and/or excuses about the story. He just reads.

No Way to Treat a Good Man
by Carl Swanson

I'll admit it, I never wanted to invite the girls to the reunions. But a lot of us fellas are alone now, and the thought did cross my mind that—well, maybe, you know. But the real problem was that we needed to have a certain number of people in order to qualify for the room with a view and a bunch of the guys don't come to the reunions anymore. A lot of them have moved to one of those retirement villages that are way outside of the area. Some have died. Anyway, attendance is down and we like that room so I figured, what the hay, those old gals could help us out with that, just like hiring them had gotten HR off our backs in the old days. If we happened to also get lucky, all the better.

If we were going to get them to come, someone had to call and invite them. Me and two other guys split up the names. I'd left messages for three women and was about to give up on the last one on my list when she answered her phone.

"Melanie?" I said. "It's Carl Swanson—from IBM." I was nervous even though I'd written out a script—you just never know what a woman might say. "We're having a former-employee reunion at the Newport Inn in three weeks. We'd sure love to see you." Though it wasn't on my script, I figured she'd want to know one of her old girlfriends would be there, so I added, "Oh, I heard, Kelly is coming."

"Carl?" she said. "Really?"

"Yeah," I said. "How are you? Come to the reunion, we can catch up."

"Uh, Carl, we were never friends, and you were a terrible boss. Kelly and I were groped, laughed at, teased and embarrassed—you encouraged it. You didn't compliment our work even when we ranked first and second in sales—for months at a time. And Carl, you never apologized."

This is just the sort of thing I didn't want to deal with.

"It was a different time," I said. "Things change."

"Carl, I don't care what happened to you. Don't you call again," she said, and hung up.

I'll tell you, women sure have gotten uppity. Yeah, there'd been teasing, but why couldn't they get over it? It was a long time ago. I try to be understanding but I've had to put up with this attitude ever since my divorce. It's gotten real hard for nice guys like me.

I dated this gal, Meg. Well, everyone can appreciate that at a certain age, the old plumbing just isn't quite the same as it used to be. I mean, I'm still a man and all, but, sometimes it just doesn't quite work. Anyway, when "that" acted up I told her the truth—that I liked young women. I figured a gal her age would understand that she's not really all that good looking anymore.

But you know what Meg does? Without missing a beat, she says, "Yeah, right, because dating a retired copier salesman who has a flat-old-man butt and skinny legs, and can't drive after dark is just what every woman in her prime dreams of."

It really hurt me when she said that. How could she be so mean? And who did she think she was anyway? She was an old woman, only six or seven years younger than me. She should have been grateful for the attention. I never called Meg again and I wouldn't call Melanie again, either.

Anyway, the night of the reception I was at the greeter's table when Kelly walked in. I waved to get her attention and thought she looked happy to see me. Let me tell ya' she looked a lot better than I'd expected. I put out my hand for her to shake and said, "Gosh, it's great to see you. You look super." I thought what the heck, I'd apologize. "You know, Kelly, I think I may need to apologize to you for the teasing that went on when we worked together."

"Oh," she says, "those were different times. Things change—I've moved on."

I'm thinking Kelly always was the

nice one but then I feel funny because she's ignoring my hand. It was sort of odd, ya' know?

Anyway, she shifts her weight and it looks as if she's going to hug me. I thought about how nice it would be to feel her breasts against me. But then she didn't hug me. She patted my shoulder with one hand and reached around me for her name tag with the other. Her breasts didn't even touch me and then she was gone, off to hug one of the younger men, who had defended the girls and called them women; leaving me, the former boss of them all, standing red-faced, with my arms spread.

And, after I'd apologized.

The bitch.

#   #   #

When Carl finishes no one moves for what seems like a long time—then everyone is rushing out the door. No one speaks to Carl, not even the coquets or his pal Lester. A couple people hand his story back to him with red edit marks on it.

Just like in his story, Carl is left red-faced and alone.

An Old Man's Poem

Harvey was an old man
who thought that he was young
he chased women half his age
and asked them out for fun

they thought that he was harmless
gave him rides to stock his larder
they'd share a glass of wine with him
but then they fled his ardor

no, no they whispered to him
a friend but nothing more
he never understood
what drove them to the door

I'm not good with women
he told everyone
no one had the heart to say
Harvey, they're too young

gals his own age liked him
made him casseroles and pie
but Harvey just kept looking
until the day he died

Claire and the Mementos

Claire and Stanley are becoming fast friends by the time Stanley's sister, who lives back east, has a stroke. Claire understands that her friend needs to go to her sister, but hates to see her leave.

Stanley plans to be gone at least six months. She's rented out her condo, moved personal items to a storage locker and taken the opportunity to clean out her closets and dispose of a lot more. At this point, all that remains are a few boxes of odds and ends to be sorted and then distributed to charities and groups that might use them. Claire enjoys doing this so Stanley drops them off at her house just before leaving town.

Claire feels her disappointment again when she opens the first box and is hit with her friend's scent. She sees the old plaid jacket Stanley always wore, next to the shirt she wore for gardening, her faded jeans, her fluffy bathrobe, and the black dress she'd wear when she wanted (or, more likely, needed) to get "all dolled up." They were too worn for resale but still had some good fabric in them; they would go to the quilters.

As she sorts things into piles for this group or that, it occurs to Claire the familiar smell might comfort, Gus, Stanley's old cat, that has been left behind with Ronnie—Stanley's sister being allergic. At the end of the day Claire takes several pieces from the quilters pile to her sewing room, and uses the fabric to make a simple quilt the size of a chair seat. Pieces of clothing are used for the top, the fluffy bathrobe serves as batting, and the least stained part of Stanley's everyday tablecloth becomes the back panel.

A few days later Claire presents the quilt to Ronnie. "It's for Gus."

"Oh, it's her clothes!" Ronnie says.

As if called, the old tom comes into the room. Claire spreads the small quilt on the chair that faces the window. The cat jumps unto it, sniffs and rearranges it slightly, makes a series of elaborate turns and lays down—purring loudly.

"Is there any fabric left?" Ronnie says.

Claire nods.

"You should make tiny quilt to put in the Memory Book," Ronnie says. "She always wore the same things. Everyone would recognize them."

The Memory Book is a collection of writings from the memoir class that is maintained by class members. When anyone from the class leaves the area, a notice is put into the book describing where and why they've gone—any cards they send to the center are put on the bulletin board for a week and then into the Memory Book.

Stanley's mini-quilt, as it would come to be known, is the first non-writing addition to the book—but not the last. After seeing it, Dolores, who is moving to Montana to live with her son because she no longer feels safe living on her own, mounts one of her doilies and puts it in the book with her writing.

Greta, who isn't leaving but wants everyone to see her work, submits two of her elaborately crocheted coasters to be placed in the Memory Book with her writing. Then Dede, who never was one to be out done, brings in her crocheted coasters; they have a pink center and protrusions off the sides that look like paws and a tail—they look like a cat's behind.

Soon there is needlepoint, hankies trimmed with fussy work, miniature sweaters, small paintings, all manor of work. Two large binders are purchased to accommodate the expanding collection. Many people ask if the women who have added their work could make things for them and several woman are asked to teach classes. After Dede's class, everyone, it seems, has cat-butt-coasters. It's all great fun.

Then Sylvia dies.

Claire thinks the woman was overbearing and entitled, but when Sylvia's daughter calls, Claire responds. It's what you do, you help the family, if you can. She meets the girl at Sylvia's house. Entering she sees the dining-room table is covered in stacks of her mother's things, several half-filled boxes are beside it.

"Are you the woman who made Stanley's mini-quilt?" Sylvia's daughter says, instead of introducing herself.

"Yes," Claire says.

"Mom thought those handicrafts were so kitschy! She always made special reference to your quilt," the girl says.

Kitschy? Claire thinks. Yes, that is what Sylvia would have said. Claire guesses Sylvia and her friends had laughed about the collection of small handiwork more than once.

"I need you to make something for my mother. Use these for the material," the girl says holding three balled up satin shirts close enough to Claire's face that she can smell the cologne that still lingers on them.

Claire struggles to maintain a neutral expression, reminding herself that the girl has just lost her mother. She looks at, but does not reach for, the shirts. They are brightly colored and clash with each another. The fabric will be difficult to work with.

"You should ask one of her friends to make something," Claire says.

"Duh, her friends don't sew or do that fussy work." Sylvia's daughter says, laughing.

"I didn't know your mother all that well ..."

"You're just making excuses," the girl says. "She knew about you and your mementos. You were in the memoir class together."

Claire is making excuses, she's reluctant to tell the girl the truth. Her mother never read anything to the class. As far as she knew, Sylvia had never written a single word, but she'd been quick to criticize the work of others. Claire is looking around the room, hoping for an easy exit, when a sandwich-sized plastic bag catches her eye and she knows—knows what she could make that would represent Sylvia. Claire reaches for the bag that is full of broken bits of costume jewelry.

"Are you throwing these away?" she says. "Can I take them?"

"I already checked, there's nothing in there worth anything," the girl says.

"Perfect. I have an idea for a memento. Can I take these?"

The girl looks suspicious. "Sure."

"The shirts, too, I'll need the shirts, too," Claire says, retrieving them from the girl. "I have your number. I'll call when it's done." Claire rushes out of Sylvia's house.

Once home Claire immediately sets to work on the collage she's envisioned. It has misshapen flowers that clash with one another and the background. The words "ensure not insure." "did you ever study the use of commas?" "no one cares about that," and "why would you write about that?" are visible through the garish background. Claire knows from the start that it will be too large to fit in the memory book, and has no idea what she will do with it, but she is driven by an unfounded certainty that completing the work is the right thing to do.

Two weeks later she shows it to Ronnie. "What were you thinking?" she says.

"Does it remind you of Sylvia?" Claire asks.

"Oh, yeah! But Claire, the colors, the insults..."

"I'm going it give it to her daughter," Claire says. "I think she'll want it."

"Oh, Claire, what if she takes offense? Claire, really, it isn't what I'd call attractive. It's...uh, harsh."

"I think it's a good memento," Claire says.

Ronnie shakes her head. "Don't be surprised if she hates it."

The next day Claire takes it to the daughter's house. "Usually the mementos go into the Memory Book with a person's writing. After I made the collage, I realized that your mother hadn't put any writing in the Memory Book, so there's no context for it," she tells the girl, not mentioning the size problem. "I thought you might want to put it with the other things you have from her."

Claire has prepared for a negative reaction but now, watching the girl look at the collage, she can't interpret her expression. As the girl turns to look at Claire there are tears in her eyes. "It's so like her —the flashy colors—the spangles—the insults. It's perfect. Thank you," she says. "What do I owe you?"

Claire is flustered. "Oh, no, I didn't make it for money. When we were talking it just appeared to me. Please, just accept it. I'm thrilled you like it."

"Oh, I didn't say I liked it," the girl says. "I said, 'it's perfect.'"

Claire feels vindicated—it is a good memento.

Mementos

After someone dies
they can become more dear
a small memento helps
to keep our memory clear

Stories of Wonder and Magic

Claire thinks the class assignment to come up with an anecdote about some wondrous or magic thing they've seen, felt, or heard about is ridiculous. She doesn't write anything and expects no one else will either.

So, she is surprised when on the day of the "wondrous" stories, many more people than usual arrive early, and most of the reading spots have been claimed. By the time she's gotten her coffee and donut and returned to the classroom two women are arguing over who should get the last spot, several others are pouting because whoever gets it, it won't be them.

When he arrives, the teacher is bombarded with complaints that there aren't enough spots for everyone. In spite of his assurances that everyone will be given an opportunity to tell their story, no matter how many classes it takes, a general discontent lingers as the readings begin.

Julie is first on the list. She has no prepared outline or story. Instead she begins a conversational telling about a time when she was suddenly drawn to a tree while taking a walk. How she saw that the tree had a beer can wedged into the place where the trunk divided into three and she found a stick and wedged it out. How she thought the tree sighed and said thank you. Julie said she patted it and said it was very welcome.

Claire is incredulous—talking with trees, what nonsense! Poor thing'll likely be taken away to a facility soon.

Julie said that on her way home she heard other trees talking. "That's her." "She can hear us." "She's the one." "She helped the tree with the can." "Shouldn't we say thank you?" "Thank you." "Thank you." "Can she really hear us?" "Yeah, see, she's smiling." "We should thank her even if she can't hear us." "Thank you." "Thank you." "Thank you."

Claire remains stoic but a couple others are leering at Julie and squirming in their seats.

Julie talks faster. She said once home she thought her belief that the trees had spoken to her may have been a sign that she was dehydrated and she drank several glasses of water. But then the next morning while she was drinking coffee in her back yard, she heard the old maple she was sitting under say, "Thank you for helping the tree with the can." She explained that she didn't know what to do so she did nothing. Then the tree said, "If you expect the gladiolas to make it through the winter, they'll need more mulch and the oak needs deep watering." It was work she planned to do that afternoon.

Someone in the class sighs loudly.

Julie talks faster yet. The morning after that, she heard the tree say, "you really can hear us" and she answered, "yes, I guess, I can."

Now whenever she sits in her yard, the tree tells her what plants need attention. Her garden, she says, is the best on the block.

Silence follows her sudden ending. Claire imagines someone will mock Julie, but no one does. And Janet, or Janice, whatever, the woman who leads the senior hikes is nodding enthusiastically and then starts into her own story. She says that she'd been sitting on her patio and a cactus wren had come close to her and squawked loudly. It had flown away and then come close again and again. She got up and followed the bird to its nest where four eggs rested. On the ground was a snake, known to raid bird's nests and eat the eggs.

The energy in the room remains high. Oh my, Claire thinks, those sighs and other signals aren't scorn, they are expressions of eagerness to tell their own story.

Janet, (Janice?), says she got a pitchfork and used it to carry the snake away from the area. Then she went to her shed, got some snake fencing and wrapped it around the tree while the wren, that had been so agitated, sat in her nest and watched her work.

She says, since then, the eggs had hatched and the birds were almost ready to leave the nest. She proclaims her belief that all of nature is connected and intended to communicate.

It seems Claire was terribly wrong about this assignment. Everyone except her has a story they want to tell.

A short dark woman breeches protocol by seizing the floor, though her name isn't on the list. Speaking over the protests she says her story is real short and she talks fast and besides, as the oldest person in the room, she should be given precedence, just in case she dies right here and now.

With no break in her speech that would allow for disagreement, she says her grandmother told her to suck on her seeds before planting them—especially vegetables. The grandmother had said it helped them grow if they knew the person who planted them. The woman says she'd always gotten better crops than her neighbors and she still does, though today her garden amounts to a few pots on the balcony of her condo. She also thanks the plants when she harvests. Though her grandmother didn't say so, she thinks they like being appreciated.

Claire likes the seed sucking story.

Then Claire's friend Ronnie, who is also not on the list, jumps up and explains how she had moved into her grandmother's house after the old woman died. One of the things she found there was her grandmother's favorite knife. Ronnie used it most days. Then, one day, she couldn't find it. She cleaned the drawer where it was kept and then searched everywhere she could image it having gone—to no avail. Weeks later, she opened that same drawer and there it sat, right on top. She says she thinks the mischief was her grandmother letting her know that she was still there with her.

Several women start talking all at once, allowing Claire the opportunity to think about her own conversations with her dead aunt and what a comfort they are. Claire wishes Maddie could see this.

And then it is as if Maddie is there, her voice is in Claire's head, saying, "I'm always here."

Claire says, "What do you make of all this?"

"You talk to me," Maddie's voice says.

"That's different," Claire says.

"Why?"

"You and I are close. Julie didn't even know those trees"

Maddie laughs. "You have a point," she says. "But what about the women and their grandmothers?"

"I like the sucking on seeds," Claire says, "but would a grandmother do that mischief with the knife?"

"Oh yeah," Maddie says, "that, and much more. You'll see." There is a pause, then Maddie says, "Claire, why don't you tell the class about our conversations?"

"I'm afraid they'll laugh at me."

"Still?" Maddie says. "Isn't it time to get over that?"

"People can be mean."

"Like you wanted to mock Julie?"

"Oh, come on! That's different! She's talking to trees. Trees! Do trees even speak English? And do trees and gladiolas speak the same language? Come on!"

The touch of Ronnie's hand on her arm interrupts her reverie. "Claire, are you all right?"

Claire is disoriented. She has never

told anyone that she talks with her dead aunt. No one.

"It was like you were a million miles away."

"Yes, I'm fine. I was just talking with my aunt Maddie," she says, feeling vulnerable.

"I talk with my husband, but only at night. It's nice when people you love hang around after they die," Ronnie says. "You know, that doesn't happen for everyone, it must be hard when someone you care about is just gone. Has it ever occurred to you that both children and old people have invisible friends? Let's go have lunch."

Ronnie's easy acceptance to her revelation puts Claire at ease.

"Mike's?"

"Mike's."

Sunrise

I sat down to write a poem
but nothing came to me
so instead I faced east
and drank a cup of tea

I was likely not the cause
but the sun rose in the sky
as it shown a bolt of light
hit me in the eye

Claire Attends an Open Mic

Claire enjoys the writing group at the Senior Center but gets tired of hearing her peers complain about the young people of today. "They're spoiled!" "I worked for everything I have." "They expect to have everything handed to them."

The remarks remind Claire of her parents, who had thought everything they'd done was a greater challenge and more of an accomplishment than anything since. How many times had she heard them say they had lived through the depression and fought in **the** war—as if there had only ever been one.

Her own generation's version, is to criticize youngsters as weak; made that way by easy lives and receiving undeserved praise. "They get awards for nothing!" more than one retired school teacher had told her.

That comment in particular rankles Claire, both for its tone and the source. Claire wants to respond to it but doesn't actually know what to say. Even if she did, she retains her childhood reluctance to talk back to a school teacher. That all changes after attending an open mic—a place where anyone could claim three minutes on a stage with a microphone to tell the world, in a poem, a story, or a song, just what they are thinking.

Claire likes that the crowd is mixed in every way. Most of the people her age arrive early, read and leave. She guesses that some want to get to a restaurant before the early-bird special stops. Likely others can't drive after dark. Though she can sympathize, she wants to tell them that leaving early is rude because it deprives those who read later of an audience.

Claire came prepared to stay late. She's eaten (and always has a protein bar in her purse, just in case she gets hungry) and has brought her special night-driving glasses. As the evening progresses, she is rewarded for her effort; the performers get younger; their work becomes more raw, more intimate; much more interesting. Claire especially likes the rap poems and the physical contortions that accompanied them.

Very late in the evening, a homely, boy stumbles onto the stage. His demeanor is shy. Claire thinks during her high school days he'd have been called a spazz. The boy starts to read but is stopped by a stutter. Claire holds her breath hoping no one picks on him.

The boy scans the room, it's unclear if he wants escape or rescue. A girl calls out, "No worries—everyone's nervous the first few times." The audience waits while he collects himself and begins again. This time he manages to recite his poem without much faltering. The audience remains attentive throughout, then applauds enthusiastically as he finishes. When he steps off the stage, two people hug him and others congratulate him for getting through the ordeal.

Claire is humbled by their kindness. She remembers that comment that so rankles her, and thinks: *Maybe those awards taught them to appreciate a person's effort, even when it fails. Maybe they've learned to value differences. Maybe they can appreciate that few of us will ever be stars; that the chorus is also important; that there is no show without an audience. Maybe they're just plain kinder and nicer than we were—or are. Maybe, they will make a better world than we did.*

Claire knows what she'll say the next time someone says, "They get awards for nothing" in front of her—even if it means sassing a school teacher.

Open Mic

he lived on the verge of tears
always set to run away
his tale told through an open mic
changed his will to stay

no one says they love me
I ache down to my bones
there's no one I can talk to
I feel so all alone

another poet answered
I feel the same as you
unprotected on my own
it happens to me too

and then another said the same
adding to the tome
and another and another
you are not alone

soon the room was full of love
a web of friendship sewn
but the evening had to end
and everyone went home

Phyllis's Story

Though they hadn't met, Claire had seen Phyllis coming and going in the community and at the senior center. She is the woman who bought Finger's condo.

Claire does not think Phyllis looks interesting. Be that as it may, it is her turn to read.

Leaving Chicago
by Phyllis Wozniak

I sat with one leg hanging over the side of the roof of the new fifteen-story, luxury-apartment building. Hailed by city planners as a sign of progress, it marked the leading edge of the gentrification that would soon overrun my north-side Chicago neighborhood, changing the environment, forcing up rents, and driving me out of the place where I'd so carefully planned to live out my retirement. Looking at the sensible, laced-up shoe on my dangling foot, I was pleased that it wouldn't fall off and hit someone below. My fine, grey hair flopped in the cold, damp wind—one more disappointment as I'd been told that as my hair turned grey it would likely coarsen and be easier to manage.

I made sure that the letter, explaining the injustice of life in general and my own special aloneness in particular, was in my purse and tightened the bag's strap across my chest to ensure it would stay with my body after I jumped—I didn't want anyone to have to work to figure out who I was.

When they heard about my death, I thought, my few friends would say it was a good thing I'd taken that trip to Peru; but a shame I'd never made it to Greece. Then they would move on. In a couple years no one would even talk about me. In five years, people would struggle to remember my name.

I pictured my only surviving relative, a nephew, and his wife, sorting my belongings and laughing at their plainness. His wife, I knew, would use my money to buy a fancy new car that she couldn't afford to maintain and their daughters would buy jeans that were overpriced and too tight. When they asked for more, my nephew would snicker and say, "It's gone. With all her skimping and saving, she didn't actually manage to accumulate much."

It made me angry to think about my precious savings being squandered. I'd lived with second hand furniture, bought my clothes on sale, and clipped coupons. I wasn't rich, but even with higher rent, I could live for some time on what I had. If I moved, my money might last longer. I could go someplace warm and sunny—Florida, or maybe California. I could make new friends, better friends. I could take a trip to Greece and Turkey too. I could do a lot of things.

Looking at my sensible shoes, I was again proud of my foresight and consideration for the safety of others, and swung my leg back inside the ledge. I could kill myself later. First I need to spend my money.

# # #

Claire gasps. "We've got to get her to

come to happy hour," she says, thinking Ronnie is next to her, but she isn't.

Looking around she sees Ronnie is somehow already on the other side of the room and introducing herself to Phyllis, shaking her hand, and pointing to Claire.

With the two of them looking at her, Claire smiles and mouths "happy hour."

Ronnie raises her thumb, nods, and mouths "done."

Rose Baldwin

Like Claire, Rose Baldwin moved from Wisconsin to the Palm Springs area. Her chapbook, The Claire Stories, was published in 2016. Her novel, Mike's Magic Burgers, was published in 2017.

Follow Rose Baldwin on Facebook
Contact: rosebaldwin253@gmail.com